This book belongs to:

_____

For Lois and Ursula,
friends for ever!

J.J.

For Mum and Dad.

S.V.

This paperback edition first published in 2013 by Andersen Press Ltd.

First published in Great Britain in 2012 by Andersen Press Ltd.,

20 Vauxhall Bridge Road, London SW1V 2SA.

Published in Australia by Random House Australia Pty.,

Level 3, 100 Pacific Highway, North Sydney, NSW 2060.

Text copyright © Julia Jarman, 2012

Illustration copyright © Susan Varley, 2012

The rights of Julia Jarman and Susan Varley to be identified as the author and illustrator

of this work have been asserted by them in accordance with the Copyright, Designs and Patents Act, 1988.

All rights reserved. Colour separated in Switzerland by Photolitho AG, Zürich.

Printed and bound in Malaysia by Tien Wah Press.

Susan Varley has used watercolour in this book.

10   9   8   7   6   5   4   3   2   1

British Library Cataloguing in Publication Data available.

ISBN 978 1 84939 727 8

This book has been printed on acid-free paper

Two Shy Pandas

Julia Jarman ❧ Susan Varley

ANDERSEN PRESS

At Number 1 Bamboo Gardens
Panda heaved a big sigh.
He longed to play with Pandora next door,
But he was much too shy.

He longed to say, "Hello, Pandora!
Please come over and play."
But when he saw Pandora . . .

. . . he was so shy he ran away!

At Number 2 Bamboo Gardens
Pandora was feeling fed up.
It wasn't much fun on a see-saw
That went down but didn't go up.

It wasn't much fun ball-bouncing
When no one bounced the ball back.

It wasn't much fun truck-racing
With nothing else on the track.

She longed to say, "Hello, Panda!"
And one day she nearly did.
But when she saw him looking at her . . .

. . . she ran away and hid.

So two little pandas stayed lonely
Too shy to say hello.
Day after lonely day went by
Until it began to snow.

Eagerly Panda rushed outside
Making snowballs was fun.
But then he thought – I need a friend.
You can't play this with one.

He threw a snowball over the fence,
And watched it fall through the air.
He waited . . . and waited . . . and then he peeped . . .

Pandora wasn't there!

Panda began to worry.
Was Pandora OK?
What if she was poorly?
What if she'd gone away?

And next door at her house,
Pandora was worried too.
"I haven't seen Panda for ages.
What if he's got the flu?"

Two very worried pandas
Wondered if they might
Be brave enough to go next door
And say, "Are you all right?"

Two very shy pandas
Opened their front doors . . .

Two brave little pandas
Hurried on chilly paws
And . . .

Two little Pandas met at last.
"Are you *really* OK?"
Two happy pandas talked very fast,
"Please come to my house and play!"

Two friendly pandas
Lonely no more.

Bounced up and down
On the see-saw.

They built a snow panda.
Working side by side.

They skated. They danced.

Then they hurried inside.

Two little pandas
Close together.
Agreed to be friends

For ever and ever.

Also illustrated by Susan Varley:

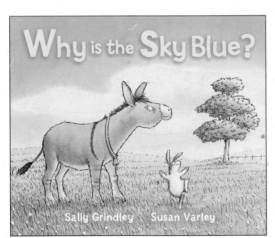

9781842705896

9781842708194

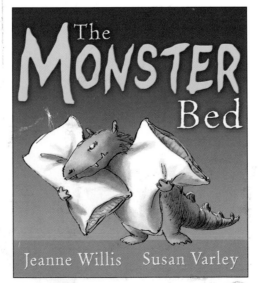

9781842702222

9781849395144